Marilyn Singer

Twenty Ways To Lose Your Best Friend

illustrated by

Jeffrey Lindberg

HARPER & ROW, PUBLISHERS

Twenty Ways To Lose Your Best Friend
Text copyright © 1990 by Marilyn Singer
Illustrations copyright © 1990 by Jeffrey Lindberg

Typography by Andrew Rhodes
1   2   3   4   5   6   7   8   9   10

First Edition

Library of Congress Cataloging-in-Publication Data
Singer, Marilyn
    Twenty ways to lose your best friend / by Marilyn Singer ;
illustrations by Jeffrey Lindberg.
        p.   cm.
    Summary: Emma loses her best friend when she votes for another
girl to get the lead role in the class play.
    ISBN 0-06-025642-7 : $. — ISBN 0-06-025643-5 (lib. bdg.) :
$
    [1. Friendship—Fiction.   2. Plays—Fiction.   3. Schools—
Fiction.]   I. Lindberg, Jeffrey K., ill.   II. Title.   III. Title:
20 ways to lose your best friend.
PZ7.S61725Tw   1990   89-36576
[Fic]—dc20   CIP
                                                         AC

Much thanks to:

Steve Aronson

Leslie Kimmelman

Jay Kerig

Oak Kerig

Asher Williams

Sandi Williams

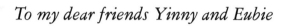

To my dear friends Yinny and Eubie

Twenty Ways To Lose Your Best Friend

1

The President of the United States made me lose my best friend.

He doesn't know he did.

And Sandy, my once best friend, doesn't know it was his fault either.

It's rotten not having a best friend. It's more alone than being alone. When you're alone, but you have a best friend, you always know you'll see her soon and then you won't be alone anymore. But when you're alone without a best friend, you feel you're going to be alone forever. Which is how I feel right now.

But I guess I'd better begin at the beginning.

It was Election Day. We were having dinner—Mom, Dad, my older brother Ronnie, and me. Mom was mad. She's mad a lot. We're all pretty used to it, especially since she isn't usually mad at us. It's other things that get her angry—things other people do. "Most people have small minds," she says.

Dad teases her sometimes. He hardly ever gets angry. He says getting angry won't help people's minds get any bigger.

Anyway, at dinnertime on Election Day Mom said, "You know, I voted this afternoon." She plopped some mashed potatoes on my plate. "While I was on line, I heard two men talking. Ooh, they made me mad." She poured some gravy on my potatoes. It splashed over the side. "One of them said to the other, 'I don't think he's as good as the other guy. But I went to school with him, so I'm voting for him.' Isn't that the dumbest thing you ever heard?"

She went over to Ronnie. He was reading a comic book. "You should vote for who you think is the best person to be president. You shouldn't vote for someone just because you know him." She dumped some potatoes on Ronnie's plate. Some of the potatoes fell off on him.

"Ma, watch out!" he yelled. He held up his comic book. It had potato lumps all over it.

Mom frowned and grabbed the comic book out of his hand. "You shouldn't be reading at the dinner table." She put the comic on an empty chair and carefully poured gravy on Ronnie's potatoes.

Next she brought the potatoes and gravy to Dad. She started to dish them

out, but he took them from her. "I'm right, aren't I, Richard?" she said.

"Yes. Ronnie shouldn't read at the table."

Mom made a face. "I meant about voting for the best person."

"Oh, well. Yes, I think you're right, Jane. But I can understand how the man you heard felt. A lot of people would vote for a friend even if he or she weren't the best person for the job."

"A lot of people have small minds," Mom said. Then she looked at me. "What do you think, Emma?" she asked.

"I don't know," I said. "I'm too young to vote for the president."

"That's true. But you never know. Someday soon you might have to choose between a friend and someone else for some job. . . . Now, eat your potatoes."

"Okay, Mom," I said.

I didn't think about what Mom said anymore that night. I didn't really think I was going to think about it anymore at all.

Boy, was I wrong.

2

"Freckle," I said.

"Spaghetti," said Sandy.

"Lavinia."

"Louis the Fourteenth."

"Louis the Fourteenth?" I gave Sandy a puzzled look.

"That's what my dad calls my brother when he gets snotty. He tries to rule the house the way Louis the Fourteenth ruled France. I think it's a good name for a cat," Sandy replied.

"Okay, write it down."

It was the Sunday after Election Day. Sandy and I were making a list of cat names. Sandy's grandmother's cat had had kittens. We were each going to take one when they were old enough to leave their mother.

Sandy and I made a lot of lists. In fact, that's how we became friends. Last year when my best friend Terry moved away, I was in a bad mood for ages. Terry and I had been friends for a long, long time. We used to do everything together. We drew pictures. We took hikes. We went ice-skating. Once while we were skating, we both fell down and cut our knees in the same place. I cried when she moved away. In school I kept staring at her empty seat. Then one day it wasn't empty anymore. A new girl was sitting there—a tall, skinny girl with long, wavy hair.

I could tell the girl was a little shy. But she tried to be friendly anyway. "Hi,

I'm Sandy McAllister," she said. "I'm glad to meet you. I just moved into the house across the street from yours." The house across the street was Terry's house. It made me mad that this Sandy McAllister person was living there now. It made me even madder that she thought she could be my friend. I gave her my killer look. I learned it from my mom. It shut Sandy up fast.

But she didn't give up trying to become my friend. The next day during art we were painting Thanksgiving scenes. Sandy and I had to push our desks together to share the paints and water.

"I'm using the brown, black, and red first." I scowled.

"Okay," she said. "I'll use the yellow and blue."

I ignored her and started to work. I was only halfway done when I stopped to look at my painting. It's going to come out good, I thought.

Sandy was staring at my picture too. "Gee, that's really nice," she told me. She sounded like she meant it. I was going to tell her thanks. But then she said, "I like the bonnets on those ladies."

"What?" I growled.

"The . . . uh . . . the bonnets on the . . . uh . . . ladies," she stammered, and pointed at my painting.

"For your information, those aren't bonnets," I said in my killer voice. "They're tail feathers. And those aren't ladies either, they're turkeys. And now I'm using the blue." I snatched it from her desk.

"I'm sorry," Sandy mumbled, and jumped up to change the water.

On the way back she tripped. The

cup of water went flying out of her hand and splashed on the floor. She slipped in the puddle and fell down.

Everyone howled. Mr. Martin, the art teacher, helped her up. She wasn't hurt, just embarrassed. "Turkey," I muttered. And everyone who heard me howled again.

After that, Sandy stayed out of my way for a while. But then one day I was sitting alone in the cafeteria. I was working in my notebook on a list. Terry and I used to make lists together all the time. We had lists of girls' names, boys' names, flowers, trees, rock groups, countries— all sorts of things. It was funny to be making lists alone now.

This time I was making a list of cars. I had eighteen types so far. I was staring down at my notebook and trying to come up with the next one when a voice said, "Pontiac."

My head shot up. Sandy was sitting across from me, reading my notebook upside down. She had a sandwich and a container of milk in front of her.

"What? What did you say?"

"Pontiac. You're listing cars and you're missing Pontiac. And Volvo. And Subaru. And—"

"SHUT UP!" I yelled. My voice was so loud, she blinked. "Shut up up up!"

Sandy swallowed hard. "I . . . I was just trying to help," she whispered. "I was just trying to be friends."

"Well, don't! Don't try. I don't want any friends. I don't need any friends." My voice was getting louder and louder, and it was starting to shake, too. Everybody was staring at me, but I couldn't stop. "Friends are stupid. Friends are crummy. Just when you think they'll always be around, they move away and leave you all alone!"

I jumped up then and grabbed at my notebook. But my hand hit the milk container and it tipped, pouring milk all over the open pages. I took one look at it and burst into tears.

Then I ran out of the room, out of the school, and into the playground. I sat there for a whole half hour. Nobody bothered me at all. When I went back to class, the other kids were just coming in.

I went to my desk. My backpack was on it, and my soggy notebook was on that. I didn't want to look at it, so I shoved it into my desk. Then I opened my backpack to take out my reading workbook and a sheet of paper fell out. There were two lists on it. The first said:

WHY FRIENDS ARE USELESS

1) They're stupid.
2) They're crummy.
3) They move away and leave you all alone.
4) ?

I felt embarrassed when I read it. Then I looked at the second list. It was much longer. It seemed serious. I sighed when I started reading it.

WHY FRIENDS ARE USEFUL

1) You can talk to a friend.
2) You can tell a friend a secret.

3) You can cry in front of a friend.

But as I kept reading, I began to smile a little.

6) A friend will give you half her tuna sandwich when your mom gives you bologna three days in a row.
7) A friend will tell you where the scary parts are in a movie she's seen and you haven't so you can hide your eyes.

And by the time I got near the end, I was wearing a big grin.

10) A friend will tell you when you have lettuce caught in your teeth.
11) You can tell a friend her nose is running.

I put the paper in my workbook and looked over at Sandy. She was grinning too.

At the end of the day, I went over to her. "Your nose is running," I said.

"Well," she answered, "I guess I'd better catch it."

Then we started to laugh. We laughed so hard, tears rolled down our cheeks.

"Want to come over to my house today?" I asked.

"Yes," she answered. And she did. And that's how we became best friends.

Sandy and I kept that list. We put it in her special blue metal box—the one with a lock. Sandy had that box out while we were making the kitten-name list.

"Lulubelle," I said.

"Purr-fect," said Sandy.

I giggled. Sandy finished writing the list, folded it, put the paper in the box, and locked it. "When we get our kittens, we'll open the box, take out the list, and pick out their names. It'll be our special Naming Ceremony."

"Great!" I agreed, excited. "And we have to swear that we won't show the list to anybody else before then."

"Okay." Sandy nodded. "I swear."

"I swear too," I said, even though I couldn't show the list to anybody anyway. I didn't have a key to the box.

We looked at each other and smiled. "I'm glad you're my best friend, Emma," Sandy told me then.

I was glad too.

3

Two days after we made up the cat name list, Sandy and I were on the bus watching Marguerite get on. We did that every morning. We didn't want to, but we couldn't help it. It was like this: Imagine you're in a room with your best friend. You have lots of interesting stuff to talk about. But the TV is on. No matter how hard you try to pay attention to your friend, you end up looking at the TV instead. That's what Marguerite was like—a TV. She pulled your eyes right to her.

Marguerite is an important part of this

story—along with the President of the U.S. (whom I've talked about) and the class play (which I'll talk about soon). But first, Marguerite.

There are some pretty girls in our fourth-grade class, like Kristi Lewis, Mary Donnelly, and Paula Ramon. But nobody is as pretty as Marguerite Perrier. She has pretty black hair, pretty blue eyes, and pretty rosy cheeks. She wears pretty pink nail polish and pretty fancy clothes. Even her name is pretty—just like the name of the fizzy water my grandma drinks. Sometimes I whisper her name over and over just because I like it so much. Marguerite Perrier. Mar-guer-eet Per-ri-ay.

But I don't like Marguerite herself as much as I like her name. She isn't a nasty person or anything; she just isn't a really nice one either. She's sort of like a princess. Which is what Sandy calls her: Princess Marguerite. If Princess Marguerite needs help on her homework or to borrow a pencil or something, she speaks to you. If she doesn't need your help, she doesn't even look your way. She's what you might call stuck-up.

There was a short time last summer when I thought Marguerite and I might get to be friends. Almost everybody I knew was on vacation, including Sandy and her family. Except us. Mom insisted we were saving for a really special trip. Ronnie asked if it was a trip to some resort he'd seen on *Lifestyles of the Rich and Even Richer*.

"No. We're not going to some silly resort. Resorts are full of lazy people. We're going to go camping in Alaska.

You can't be lazy in Alaska," Mom said.

"You can just freeze to death," I muttered.

"Or get eaten by a bear," added Ronnie.

"Nonsense. You'll love Alaska—when we get there in a couple of years. Stop having such a small mind."

So I was stuck here. And it turned out Marguerite was too. One day she came over to me at the neighborhood pool. "Hi. You're Emma, right? Can I sit with you?" she asked.

"Sure," I answered. I was surprised, but kind of pleased too.

Marguerite smiled and sat down. She told me about all the acting, dancing, and singing lessons she was taking and the ones she wanted to take and how she was going to be a big movie star someday. I told her how I was going to go to Alaska. We had a pretty good time.

I should have figured out right then that Marguerite was only hanging out with me because her friends were away. But I didn't figure it out for five whole days, till her friends came back and Marguerite stopped sitting with me at the pool. She stopped talking to me too for the rest of the summer. Except once when she wanted to borrow my towel.

I felt hurt. When Sandy got back, she said, "You can't be friends with somebody like Princess Marguerite. So don't even try."

"I won't. Not ever again," I replied.

That Tuesday morning, when Sandy and I were watching Marguerite get on the bus, I still didn't want to be friends with her. And I still couldn't help watching her.

She looked especially pretty that day.

23

She was wearing a blue dress that matched her eyes and a blue ribbon in her hair that matched the dress. "Boy, she really looks like a princess today," I said.

"That's because she's trying out for the class play."

"The class play? Are tryouts today?"

Sandy rolled her eyes at me. "Didn't you hear Ms. Wood tell us that last week?"

I shrugged. I didn't much care about the class play. I always ended up being an elf, a snowflake, or tooth decay. I liked painting the scenery more. That's what Sandy and I did together last year.

"I hope we get to do some pretty scenery this year," I said. "Something sparkly, maybe. Don't you?"

Sandy gave me a funny little smile.

"Why are you smiling like that?" I asked.

24

"No reason." Sandy shrugged, wiping the smile off her face.

"Okay," I said, believing her.

We went back to watching Princess Marguerite until we got to school.

4

The class play was called *Mighty Mush*. It was about this dumb, skinny dog named Mush who couldn't do anything right until the Wish Fairy came along to help him. Then he became Mighty Mush, smart and strong, able to leap tall buildings in a single bound, and stuff like that. When the evil Swinella made all of Santa's reindeer fall asleep on Christmas Eve, dumb Mush became Mighty Mush. He pulled Santa's sleigh all by himself and defeated Swinella.

The play was supposed to be a comedy. One of the jokes was when Santa said,

"Mush, Mush!" But nobody got it. Ms. Wood had to explain it to us. She said "Mush" is what people say to sled dogs when they want them to pull the sled, and it's also the dog's name in the play. "You have to say the first 'Mush' as though it were the word 'Go' and the second just as if it were a name like Spot. '*Go*, Spot!' '*Mush*, Mush!' See? It's funny."

I didn't think it was. Neither did anybody else. I didn't think the play was very good either. But I could tell some of the other kids did. They were the kids who hoped to get one of the good parts in it.

There were a lot of parts in this play. Teachers always pick plays with lots of parts so everybody will get a chance to be in it, whether he or she wants to or not. But there are also only a few *good* parts in each play. This one had four—Mush, Swinella, Santa, and the Wish Fairy. I wouldn't have minded playing Swinella, but I knew Jackie Dixey with her cackling laugh would get it and I would end up playing an elf again.

During reading we silently read the play instead of a story in our readers. I kept trying to catch Sandy's eye to let her know what I thought of it. But she didn't look up once.

At lunchtime, which was before try-outs, I asked her what *she* thought of the play. She said she thought it wasn't bad. That surprised me, but I said that I guessed it was better than last year's play, *Look Out, Teeth!* "We could do a good job on Santa's workshop," I went on. "We could paint fake shelves with toys on them."

Sandy gave me another funny smile

and suggested we work on our latest list—Fifteen Ways to Eat Pizza.

When we got back to our classroom after lunch, Ms. Wood was all ready for us. On the board she'd written: Mush, Santa, Swinella, the Wish Fairy, Mrs. Claus, Dasher, Dancer, Head Elf. "Those are the *speaking parts*," she said. "They have *lines* to say. . . . Now, this is how I run tryouts. When I point to one of these parts, you raise your hand if you want to try out for it. I will write down the name of everybody who wants to try out for that part. Then I will call each name alphabetically. When I call your name, you'll come up to the front of the room and read the part. When all the people have finished trying out for that part, they will leave the room. The rest of the class will vote by a show of hands for the best person."

Immediately, everyone started to buzz. None of our other teachers had ever done that. Our other teachers had tryouts all right, but *they* picked the best person for each part. This was the first time we would get to do it. Some kids thought it was a great idea. Others didn't. Marguerite was one of the ones who didn't. I could tell by the frown on her face. But she didn't say anything to Ms. Wood.

A lot of kids wanted to play Mush. We listened to all of them try out. Some were okay. One was really bad. And a couple of them were very good. I thought Katie Willis was the best. So did most of the other kids, because she won.

Ms. Wood said that the people who tried out for Mush and didn't get the part could try out for the other roles if they wanted to. Jimmy Whaley, the other kid who'd been good as Mush, tried out for Santa Claus. He was even better in that part. So this time I picked him. But he didn't win. Frankie Moffo did. Frankie wasn't nearly as good as Jimmy, but he was twice as fat, and that's why he won. Even Sandy voted for him. However, that's probably because she can't stand Jimmy Whaley. He's always calling her Stork—I guess because she's tall and skinny like that bird. It wouldn't bother me if Jimmy called me that, but Sandy hates it.

Jackie Dixey got the part of Swinella. Nobody else even tried out for it.

The Wish Fairy was next on the list. "All right," said Ms. Wood. "If you want to try out for this part, raise your hand."

Marguerite's hand shot up right away. So did a couple of the other girls', but I could tell from the expression on Princcss Marguerite's face that she didn't think they were any competition. I turned to Sandy to share what I thought of her, and that's when I got a shock. Sandy wasn't looking at me. She was looking right at Ms. Wood and her hand was raised high in the air. My shy best friend had been planning all along to try out for a big part in the class play and she hadn't even told me!

I was bugged. And I was going to tell her so. But then she turned to me with her face so shiny and excited, I had to grin. "I wanted to keep it a surprise," she whispered. "Wish me luck."

"Good luck," I whispered back.

Four girls in all were trying out for the Wish Fairy. Sandy was third. Marguerite was last. Marguerite was smiling, but underneath I knew she had to be nervous too. Even though Sandy was shy, more people liked her than Marguerite. I hoped more than anything that Sandy was going to play the Wish Fairy and that Princess Marguerite would end up as a snoring reindeer. And it seemed like it might happen too, especially when the first two girls weren't so hot.

I gave Sandy a thumbs-up sign when she stood up at last. I gave her a big smile when she reached the front of the room. Then she began to read, and it was hard to keep smiling.

Sandy, my best, best, best friend Sandy, was awful. She stuttered and stumbled and tripped over the words. She hunched her shoulders and scrunched up her neck. Instead of acting like the Wish Fairy, she acted more like somebody who badly needed the Wish Fairy's help.

"How was I?" she asked when she got back to her seat.

"Uh, interesting," I answered.

"Huh? What does that mean?"

But I didn't have to answer—at least not then—because Marguerite had just gotten up to read. The minute she opened *her* mouth, mine dropped open. She was good. She was so good, I forgot she was Marguerite. She was so good, I expected any minute she was going to grow wings and fly around the room, granting everybody his or her favorite wish.

I was so thrilled by her performance that I forgot all about Sandy. But not for long. Because one minute after Marguerite finished, Ms. Wood said, "All right. You four girls leave the room so the rest of the class can vote."

That's when I realized I had a horrible

problem. Who should I vote for? Sandy, who was my best friend but a terrible actress? Marguerite, who was a terrific actress but somebody I didn't like? I wished the Wish Fairy would show up for real and fly me to Alaska right then and there.

I looked around the room for help. But instead of the Wish Fairy, I saw the President of the United States and I remembered what Mom had said the week before, on Election Day. I was certain I didn't want to have a small mind. So I knew how I had to vote.

The trouble was I was afraid of what would happen if Sandy found out. I decided I wouldn't ever, ever tell her.

And I didn't. Somebody else did.

5

Sandy didn't find out right away that I'd voted for Marguerite. What she did find out in less than five minutes was that she'd lost by only one vote.

"One vote," she sighed on the bus ride home. "One measly vote."

I sat there feeling weird. It was one thing for your vote to help somebody win, and another thing for it to make somebody lose. My measly vote had made my best friend Sandy lose. And now she was looking at me with big, sad eyes, feeling rotten about losing, waiting for me to say something to make her feel better. I couldn't tell her the truth. But I didn't want to lie either.

"Well." I cleared my throat. "Well, losing by . . . uh . . . one . . . uh . . . vote isn't so . . . uh . . . bad. It, uh, means a lot of, uh, people voted for you." So far so good.

"Yeah—but not enough people." Sandy sighed again.

"Well, you'll . . . uh . . . still be in the play. Blitzen isn't . . . uh . . . a bad part. And you'll be able to work on the—"

"Who voted for me?" Sandy interrupted.

"—scenery," my voice squeaked. I swallowed. Some saliva went down the wrong way, and I started to cough. I coughed for a long time, way after I needed to keep coughing.

"Are you okay?" Sandy asked, patting me on the back.

"Fine. I'm fine." I looked out the bus window as we pulled up to a stop. Quinton Street. We were only halfway home. I knew I couldn't keep coughing the whole rest of the way. So I quit.

"Feel better now?" Sandy asked.

I nodded, hoping she'd forget what she'd asked me before.

She didn't. "So, who voted for me?" she repeated.

I sighed. "I, uh, I didn't really notice." That wasn't a lie either. I hadn't noticed—much.

"You didn't notice anybody?"

"Well, uh . . ." I stuttered out a few names, ending with Jimmy Whaley.

"Jimmy Whaley!" Sandy exclaimed. "Jimmy Whaley hates me."

Bingo! I'd said the magic name. If I

could get Sandy to talk about Jimmy Whaley, we wouldn't have to talk about the tryouts. "No, he doesn't," I said eagerly. "He teases you, but that doesn't mean he hates you. I think he likes you. I think he thinks you're nice."

"No, he doesn't. I saw him yesterday when I was at the supermarket with my mom. You know what he did? He stuck a label on my back that said '25¢.' I didn't know why everybody was laughing at me until my mom saw the label and took it off. And last week . . ."

Hooray! I've done it, I cheered silently as the bus stopped again and more kids began to file off. I've gotten Sandy to stop talking about the tryouts. We're almost home and everything's going to be all right.

Then I looked up and saw Marguerite smiling at me.

"Kristi told me," she said. "I want to thank you. . . . And Sandy, I think it's great that you don't mind. You know, I'm having a party on Sunday afternoon. Maybe you'd both like to come."

"Uh, maybe," I stammered.

"Great!" She smiled again and got off the bus.

"What was all that about?" asked Sandy. "Why was she thanking you?"

"For, uh, for lending her my, uh, pen," I said. So much for telling the truth.

"Oh," said Sandy. But then, a moment later, "What did she mean that it's great that I don't mind?"

"Well, it was, uh, really *your* pen. The, uh, red one you lent me. I told Marguerite that."

"Oh." Sandy frowned a little. "I can't

believe she invited us to her party because you lent her my pen."

"I can't either," I said quickly. "Maybe some of her other friends are sick or something."

"Well, I'm not going. Are you?"

"Definitely not," I said, breathing kind of funny.

I was happy when the bus finally let us off at our bus stop and my breathing wasn't funny anymore.

6

It wasn't hard to tell when Sandy found out. Wednesday afternoon at my house we were having a great time working on our latest list: Ten Things We Hate About Older Brothers. Thursday morning at the bus stop she wouldn't even look at me. She just stared across the street with her face as stiff as one of the wooden masks Mom has hanging over her desk.

Oh no, I said to myself when I saw her. Who did it? Who told her? "What's wrong?" I asked, hoping maybe I was wrong.

She wouldn't answer me.

"Come on, Sandy. I'm your friend."

She turned her head slowly and stared at me as if I were a germ. "My *friend?*" she said. Her voice was colder than my doctor's stethoscope. "*My* friend. That's funny. I thought you were somebody else's friend. Somebody whose name begins with *M* and ends with *eat.*"

"That's not true. I'm not friends with—"

Sandy went right on, "Somebody you picked to play the Wish Fairy instead of the person you said was your *best* friend."

"I didn't!" I yelled, so loudly that Sandy blinked, then looked confused.

"You didn't?" she said. "You didn't vote for Marguerite instead of me?"

I bit my lip. "Well, I did. But it's not what you think—"

"What I think!" Sandy shouted. "What I think is I never want to talk to you again, Emma Ames. Never ever!" She turned and stomped up the steps of the bus, which had just arrived, and sat down next to Jimmy Whaley. I sat down across the aisle.

"Hey, Stork, how come you're not sitting with your good buddy?" Jimmy asked with a goofy grin.

"Shut up," she snapped at him. "You shut up!" She took out a book and started to read it.

Jimmy's eyes got big. He looked over her head at me.

I lowered my eyes so he couldn't see that they were wet. "Yeah, Jimmy, shut up," I said. But I don't think he heard me.

* * *

By the end of the day, everybody knew that Sandy and I weren't friends anymore. At lunchtime she sat way across the room with a bunch of other girls. In gym she didn't pick me for her team. On the bus ride home, she laughed when mean Bobby Deacon tripped me on the way to my seat. And she hurried off at our stop without even saying good-bye.

I walked home feeling bad. By dinner I felt even worse.

"Do you know how much time the average American family spends in front of the TV every day?" Mom asked. She slipped a hamburger in the roll on Ronnie's plate.

Ronnie flipped a page of his comic and didn't answer.

"Six hours! Can you imagine? Six hours in front of a TV!" She grabbed the comic out of Ronnie's hand and dropped it on the floor. "No wonder there are so many small minds around. Think of all the other things a family could do in six hours. Read, play games, exercise, talk . . ."

"Have food fights. Put bugs in each other's beds," Ronnie muttered.

"What was that?" said Mom.

"Nothing," Ronnie answered.

Mom came over to me. "Families should talk more. Talking is important. Do you want another hamburger, Emma? . . . Why, Emma, you haven't even eaten your first one. Are you sick?"

I shook my head.

"Is something else wrong, Emma?" Dad asked in a soft voice. "You've been awfully quiet tonight."

I started to shake my head again. But I ended up nodding it instead. "Yes, something's wrong. Something's *very* wrong," I said. And I burst into tears.

It took a while before I could finally tell them what had happened. "Two days ago we had tryouts for the class play. I remembered what you said, Mom, about not having a small mind and voting for the best person and not your friend. And that's what I did."

"Oh, Emma. That's wonderful," Mom said. "It means you have a big mind. A very big mind!"

"Who was the friend?" asked Dad. "The person you didn't vote for?"

"Sandy," I said.

"Sandy!" Dad raised his eyebrows.

"Sandy!" Ronnie yelled. "But she's your best friend!"

I shook my head. "Not anymore. She found out I didn't vote for her, and now she hates me."

"I don't blame her," said Ronnie. "If I were her, I'd hate you too."

"Ronnie, be quiet," Dad told him, and he shut up. "Did you try to explain to Sandy why you didn't vote for her?" he asked me.

"I tried," I said. "But she wouldn't listen. Now I don't know what to do." I looked at Mom.

But she wasn't looking at me. "Hmmm, that must be the reason," she said to herself.

"The reason for what?" asked Dad.

Mom looked up. "The reason why Nancy McAllister gave me the cold shoulder today."

"Oh no!" I exclaimed. Nancy McAllister is Sandy's mom—my mom's best friend. They're on a lot of committees together and they talk on the phone all the time. They even bought each other's junk at the flea market the library had to raise money for new books.

"Don't worry," Mom assured me. "Now that I know what happened, I'll talk to Nancy. She'll talk to Sandy and make her understand. You'll see—by tomorrow night, you and Sandy will be best friends again." She gave me a big smile.

I couldn't help smiling back. Whew, I thought. Everything's going to be all right. Mom's going to fix everything.

Some people never learn.

7

I couldn't wait for Friday to end. I was sure everything would be all right by dinnertime. Mom had told me it would be. I made up a poem about it. I hardly ever write poems, but this one just popped into my head. It went:

> Friday morning
> I feel bad
> Friday morning
> I feel sad
> But Friday night
> I will feel dandy

'Cause I'll be friends again
with Sandy

I wrote down the poem in the back of my list notebook. Every time I saw Sandy pretending not to see me or joking with somebody else, I read the poem. It was like a magic spell. It made me feel better.

I read the poem again on the cafeteria line. Sandy was sitting with the same bunch of girls she'd sat with the day before. They were laughing about something, and Sandy was laughing the hardest.

"Pink," I heard somebody say, interrupting my thoughts.

"No, blue," said somebody else.

"Let's ask Emma," a third voice put in. "What do you think, Emma?"

I closed my notebook with a bang and looked up. Marguerite was smiling at me. Her friends Kristi and Jeanine were with her.

"About what?" I asked.

"About my costume for the play. Should the Wish Fairy wear a pink leotard or a blue one?"

"Blue," I said. "Like the sky."

"See?" said Jeanine.

"Like the sky," repeated Marguerite. "That's nice. Maybe I should wear my mother's star necklace."

I nodded. "And put glitter in your hair."

"Ooh, glitter!" said Kristi. "That'll look so pretty."

"Move it, girls. You're holding up the line," said Ms. White, who serves the food.

Jeanine, Kristi, and Marguerite had sandwiches with them, so they just got juice. I was getting lunch that day. It was something called "Tuna Melange." I once asked Dad what that meant. "Leftovers," he said.

Jeanine frowned at my tray. "You're eating that yuck?" she said.

"Don't be rude, Jeanine," said Marguerite. "Come sit with us, Emma," she said to me. "And we can talk more about my costume. You have such good ideas."

"Well, uh, I don't know. . . ." I'd never sat with Marguerite and her friends before. I looked over at Sandy. She was still laughing.

"Okay," I said.

We walked across the room with our trays. Just as we passed Sandy's table, she looked up at us. Her face got all pinched. She turned her head quickly away.

"Um, I think I've got to go to the girls' room," I said. I put down my tray, grabbed my notebook, and hurried out of the cafeteria. I went into the girls' room, opened my notebook, and read my poem five times in a row. Then I went back to the cafeteria.

"Ballet slippers," Jeanine was saying.

"No, satin shoes with sequined bows," Kristi disagreed.

"What do you think, Emma?" asked Marguerite.

"Ballet slippers," I said, hating to agree with Jeanine again.

"See?" she said.

"That lace up your ankle."

"Ooh, pretty!" Kristi said.

Marguerite nodded, smiling. "Emma,

you are so smart. You'll have to sit with
us every day."

I didn't tell them that I was one hundred percent sure that I wasn't going
to be sitting at their table ever again.

Mom wasn't home yet when I got
there. Dad wasn't home yet either. But
Ronnie was. He's supposed to baby-sit
me when Mom and Dad aren't there.
I've told them I'm too old for a baby-

sitter. Ronnie has too. But they won't listen to either of us.

So there was Ronnie, reading a comic book. "Will Mom be home soon?" I asked him. I was nervous. My voice was squeaky.

He shrugged.

"I hope she is."

He shrugged again.

I made a face at him and started to leave the room.

"Emma!" Ronnie called out.

I turned around.

"I don't think you should count on Mom too much."

"What do you mean?"

"To fix things up with you and Sandy."

I put my hands on my hips. "Why not?"

"Remember a few years ago I had to

do a report on my favorite animal and I did it on a dragon? It was a good report, but my teacher, Mr. Cade, gave me a D on it because it wasn't about a real animal."

"No, I don't remember," I said. "What happened?"

"Well, Mom said Mr. Cade was wrong and she'd tell him that. 'You'll see. After I talk with him, he'll change your grade,' she said. Well, she went to talk with him, and he changed it all right. He changed it to an F!"

"This isn't the same thing," I said loudly.

Ronnie shrugged. "Okay," he said, and went back to his comic.

I stuck my tongue out at him, hurried up to my room, and sat down on my bed to wait for Mom to come home. I didn't have to wait long. As soon as I heard the front door slam, I rushed right downstairs.

"Mom!" I called, running up to her. "Mom! Is everything okay? Did you talk to Sandy's mom? Can I call Sandy right now?"

Mom didn't answer me right away. First she put down her bag on the hall table. Next she took off her coat and hung that carefully in the closet. Then she smoothed out her ruffled hair. At last she turned to me. "Yes, I talked to Nancy McAllister," she said slowly. "And I think that Nancy McAllister has the smallest mind in New York State!" With a toss of her head, she walked into the kitchen.

I stood there watching her go. Then I saw Ronnie next to me. He had the biggest I-told-you-so look on his face.

"Stuff it, Ronnie Ames!" I shouted. I ran past him up the stairs to my room, ripped my poem out of my notebook, and tore it into a hundred teensy-weensy pieces.

8

"Dress shoes," Mom was grumbling. "I hate dress shoes. They're not comfortable. They're not practical. And they cost too much money. Why can't I wear my sneakers?"

I didn't answer her. I was mad at her. Last night I'd been angry, but I hadn't said anything. Today I was still angry. She'd promised to fix things with Sandy and she'd made them worse. And now I had to go shopping with her. I hate shopping with Mom because she hates shopping. When I need clothes, Dad usually takes me. He likes shopping. He says he could spend all day in the mall just watching the people.

But this time Dad was busy. I needed a new winter coat and Mom needed a new pair of shoes for a wedding she and Dad were going to.

"Look at this pair," Mom said, pointing to some very high heels. We had already bought my coat, and we were in the shoe department. "Who on earth could walk in these? The only thing you can do with a shoe like this is use it to plant seeds." She picked up one shoe and pretended she was poking holes in the ground with the heel.

I couldn't take it anymore. "Mom!" I blurted out. "What am I supposed to do about Sandy now? You were supposed to fix things."

"It's not my fault that Nancy McAllister is so small minded." She paused, then said, "You'll just have to wait until Sandy realizes you were right."

"What if she doesn't?" I asked.

"If she doesn't, you'll just have to find some other friend."

"But I don't want some other friend. I want Sandy!" My voice was loud.

A couple of people turned to look at us. I got embarrassed and stared down at my feet. A salesman hurried over. "May I help you?" he asked.

"Yes," Mom said, looking him right in the face. "You can tell me if this pair of shoes comes with a matching pair of crutches."

"I beg your pardon?"

"Never mind." Mom put down the shoe she'd been holding. "Come on, Emma, let's go have some lunch. Things always look better after lunch."

We went to Trendy's for lunch. I love Trendy's. They have big hamburgers and really thick shakes. Mom almost never takes me there, though. She calls Trendy's "Heart Attack Heaven." She claims the food they serve isn't good for you. "It clogs up your plumbing," she says. She thinks Ronnie and I should eat more stuff like broccoli, beans, and oatmeal. Not too long ago Ronnie dumped a bowl of oatmeal into the sink and it wouldn't go down. *"Oatmeal* clogs up your plumbing," he told Mom. I laughed a lot, but she didn't think it was very funny.

But this time Mom didn't say one bad thing about Trendy's. She even let me get French fries with my burger and shake. She got a fish sandwich, a salad, and tea. We took our food to a table near the window. I wanted to look outside and think about how to make Sandy my friend again.

But Mom wouldn't let me. She wanted to talk. First she told me how mad she was at the Library Committee because they turned down her idea for Children's Book Week. Her idea was that the librarians should dress up as characters from famous children's books and take the kids on a trip through Bookland. "They said it was too much work. So we're having Mr. Bookworm again, for the sixth year in a row. I'm sick to death of Mr. Bookworm."

I was sick to death of him too, but I didn't say anything.

Then she changed the topic to Thanksgiving and how people don't even know what the holiday means—they just use it as an excuse to stuff themselves. "I'm not going to let our guests do that this year. I'm not going to make as much food."

"You won't have to. The McAllisters won't be coming," I muttered. I didn't think she had heard me. But she had.

"Look, Emma, I know you like Sandy and you want her to be your friend again. But there are other people you can be friends with too. Just like there are other people I can be friends with besides Nancy McAllister," she said loudly, as if she were making an announcement.

"Oh, yeah?" I blurted out. "What other people? Who?"

"There are lots of people. There are people everywhere you can be friends with. For example, that girl over there."

"Huh? What girl?" I asked, confused.

"The one who's smiling at us."

I turned my head, and then I saw

whom Mom was looking at. Oh no. It figures, I said silently. It was Marguerite. Kristi was with her, and they were both heading our way.

"Hi, Emma," Marguerite said when she got to our table. "Guess what? I got a new leotard and new ballet slippers. Sky-blue ones that lace up the ankle. Just like you suggested."

"She's going to look *s-o-o-o* pretty," said Kristi.

Marguerite smiled at her just the way a princess would smile at her lady-in-waiting.

"That's nice," I said. I wished they'd both go away.

But then Mom said, "Aren't you going to introduce us, Emma?"

"Oh. Yeah. Mom, this is Prin— I mean Marguerite. And Kristi. Marguerite, Kristi, this is my mom."

They smiled at each other. Then Marguerite said, "We've got to go. My mother and I need to get new dresses. We don't want to wear last year's dresses for Thanksgiving." She nodded at a table in the corner. A blond woman was sitting there, sipping a soda. She looked just like a grown-up Marguerite.

"I hope you know that Thanksgiving is not about new dresses," Mom said. "Or about stuffing ourselves with food."

I rolled my eyes. Kristi saw me and giggled.

But Marguerite said, "Oh, no. I know all about the real meaning of Thanksgiving. My family has a lot to be thankful for. My great-great-great-great-grandparents escaped to this country during the French Revolution. They would have been killed in France."

"Why?" I asked. I was curious, even though I didn't want to be.

"They were—aristocrats," Marguerite said. She didn't stick her nose in the air, but she might as well have.

"Yeah? Were they the King and Queen of France?"

"The King and Queen of France were decapitated." Marguerite sounded just like Ms. Wood. I waited for her to ask, "Who knows what *decapitated* means?"

She didn't. But Kristi answered as if she had. "*Decapitated* means they had their heads chopped off."

Marguerite smiled at her the way Ms. Wood does when someone gives a correct answer.

"So, who were your great-great-whatever-grandparents?" I asked.

"The Duke and Duchess of Perrier," Marguerite announced proudly.

"How interesting," Mom said. "If they'd stayed in France and not been killed, you might have been a French duchess yourself."

"Instead of a North American princess," I muttered.

"What was that, Emma?" Mom asked.

"Nothing."

"We really do have to go," Marguerite said. "It's been nice to meet you, Mrs. Ames. I'll see you tomorrow at the party, Emma. Don't forget—it's at two o'clock."

"Oh, the party. Right. Well, actually, Marguerite, I don't think—" I began.

But Mom interrupted: "Why, Emma. You didn't tell me you were invited to a party tomorrow." She gave me a funny look.

"I guess I . . . uh . . . forgot."

"I hope that doesn't mean she can't come," said Marguerite.

"Not at all. Two o'clock, you said? I can drive you myself, Emma."

"Oh, excellent," Marguerite said, and she and Kristi left.

I gave Mom a killer look mean enough to burn Trendy's burgers. But she didn't even notice. "See?" she said. "I told you there were lots of people you could be friends with. Look, you've made a new friend already." She stood up. "Now I'm ready to face those shoes." She marched away.

I slapped my forehead. I could think of only one thing worse than going to Marguerite's party: being decapitated.

9

I was staring at my socks. I'd been staring at them for at least a minute. Maybe I could cut holes in them, I thought. Yeah, that's it. I'll throw all my other socks into the hamper and tell Mom my only clean ones have holes in them and I can't go to Marguerite's party with holey socks. But I knew as soon as I thought it it was a dumb idea. "No one will notice your socks," Mom would say.

I sighed. I was stuck going to Marguerite's party no matter what.

I wondered what Sandy was doing today. Marguerite had invited her to the party too, but I was positive she wasn't coming. Maybe she was going to a movie. Or for a hike. Maybe she was working on a new list without me. A tear rolled down my cheek.

"Emma, are you ready yet?" Mom called.

I brushed the tear away. "Almost," I called back.

"You've been saying that for the past half hour!" I heard her start to come up the stairs.

Then the telephone rang and she went back down to answer it.

Slowly I began to put on my socks.

A few minutes later Mom came into my room. She looked me up and down. "Well, once you have your shoes on, you'll look very nice."

"Thanks," I mumbled, picking up a sneaker.

Then she said, "That phone call was for you."

I looked up. "For me? Who was it? Marguerite, calling off the party?" I asked hopefully.

"No. It was Sandy."

I dropped the sneaker. "Sandy? Is she still on the phone? Does she want to talk to me?" I grabbed my sneakers and put them on so fast, I stuck the left one on my right foot and the right one on my left foot. I dashed for the door.

"Hold it, Emma. She's not on the phone anymore. I told her you were busy and couldn't talk now."

"You did what? Sandy called me after not talking to me for a week and you said I was busy!"

"You *were* busy. You were getting ready for a party. And if we don't leave this minute, you're going to be late!"

"You didn't tell her *that*, did you? You didn't tell her I'm going to Marguerite's party?" I wailed.

"No, I didn't—and if you'll stop yelling, I'll give you the message Sandy said to deliver."

I shut my mouth tight.

"That's better. Sandy said to tell you her grandmother's giving away the kittens today and you should pick yours up at Sandy's house at five o'clock. Now put your shoes on the right feet and let's go."

All the way to Marguerite's house I was excited. Sandy had called me! Sandy had asked me to come over! I was going to get my kitten and get back my best friend—all on the same day. All I had to do was get through Marguerite's party. And that wouldn't be so bad, now, would it?

10

"Okay, she's ready. You can start the music," Jeanine announced, peeking behind the curtain that was really a bedspread.

Marguerite's mother pressed a switch on a tape recorder. A high man's voice came on singing a silly song about some girl who was lovely to look at and delightful to know. The curtain opened, and out came Marguerite wearing three petticoats, one of them on her head like a bride's veil.

Everyone applauded except me. We were playing a game called Fashion Show.

We were supposed to pick out and put on clothes from a big trunk. Whoever had the best outfit won. I thought it was the stupidest game I'd ever played. I also thought Marguerite's party was the second-worst party I'd ever gone to (the worst was last Easter at school, when I sat down on a bunch of melted jelly beans and couldn't get up from my seat). All of Marguerite's games were dumb ones, and even her food was weird.

"Marguerite has the best parties," Greta, the girl sitting next to me, said.

I looked at Greta as if she were crazy. "You think this is a good party?" I said.

But she didn't hear me. "You're so lucky to be Marguerite's friend," she went on. "I wish I were." She sighed the biggest sigh.

"You're not her friend?" I asked, not bothering to tell Greta I wasn't Marguerite's friend either.

"No. I'm her cousin. She has to invite me to her parties. But she doesn't have to be my friend."

"All right now. Who's next? Greta?" called Ms. Perrier.

"All the girls in my class would be jealous of me if she were my friend. They think Marguerite's wonderful. I bet all the girls in your class are jealous of you," Greta finished. Then she got up to take her turn.

We played Fashion Show some more until everybody had gone and Marguerite had won, just the way she'd won every other game at her party. Just when I thought I couldn't stand being there another minute, the doorbell rang.

A few seconds later, Marguerite's dad

stuck his head in the room. "Emma's mother is here."

"Oh, good!" I jumped to my feet. "I mean, oh well. I guess I have to go now."

"But you haven't had any cake yet," said Ms. Perrier. She pointed to the thing she was slicing. It was gray with tiny little seeds all over it. "It's a poppy-seed cake."

"That's okay. I have to eat dinner soon," I said, trying not to make a face, and I rushed up the stairs.

"Hi, Mom. I'm all ready to go," I greeted her.

But before I could leave, Marguerite appeared. "Emma, I hardly had a chance to talk to you," she said. "I hope you had a good time." She put her arm over my shoulder.

"I liked the punch," I told her, and started out the door.

But Marguerite didn't take her arm off me. "Before you go, I want to ask you about my tiara."

"Your what?"

"Tiara. It's a little crown like ballet dancers wear. Don't you think the Wish Fairy should wear one?"

"Sure. That would look nice."

"The problem is they're kind of expensive."

"You could make one," I said.

"That's a great idea. But I don't have much talent for making things. Maybe you could help me."

"Sure," I said, without thinking.

"Oh, that would be excellent," said Marguerite. She took her arm off me at last.

I grabbed Mom's arm and hurried out the door.

* * *

All the way home I could hardly sit still. I told Mom she wasn't driving fast enough. She told me her driving was just fine. Finally she pulled the car into our driveway. I threw open my door.

"Be back in time for dinner," she called after me as I ran across the street to Sandy's house. I rang the bell and wiggled from one foot to another until Sandy's older brother, Malcolm, opened the door.

"Hi, Malcolm," I said with a huge grin. Malcolm's a big pest. I always end up telling him to get lost—if Sandy hasn't told him first. But today I was glad to see him.

"What are *you* doing here?" he asked. "Sandy told me she never wanted to see you again."

"Sandy's come to her senses," I said. I pushed past him into the house and headed straight for Sandy's room.

Her door was closed. I didn't knock. Sandy and I never knocked on each other's doors. I just opened it quickly and stood in the doorway.

Sandy was sitting on the floor, laughing. In front of her was the blue metal box where she kept our list of names. Two kittens were rolling around next to the box. They kept banging into it, but they didn't seem to mind.

"Hi, Sandy. I'm here!" I said loudly and eagerly.

Sandy stopped laughing and looked up. "Hello, Emma," she said with a frown. "Is it five o'clock already?"

I got confused. Sandy didn't seem very pleased to see me. But I thought maybe she was just tired or something. "The kittens have gotten so big," I said, coming all the way into the room. It was over a month since I'd seen them—soon after they were born.

Suddenly, a third kitten popped up from behind the box. "Oh, Sandy!" I exclaimed. "Did you get two kittens?"

"No, that one's mine," somebody said. I looked up. It was Paula, one of the girls Sandy'd been sitting with in the cafeteria. She was across the room on Sandy's bed, and she had a piece of paper in her hand. "Her name is Lulubelle."

"Lulubelle?" I said slowly.

"Uh-huh. And Sandy's is named Louis the Fourteenth."

"Louis the Fourteenth?" I repeated.

"Yes. What are you going to name yours? There are some really good names on this list."

I turned and stared at Sandy. "You swore," I choked. "You swore you wouldn't show it to anybody!"

Sandy didn't say anything. She just stared back like she didn't care what she'd done.

I snatched up my kitten. I'd never give her a name from that list now. Never ever.

"Oh, do you have to go, Emma? Can't you let them play together a little longer?" said Paula. "They're having so much fun."

Suddenly I stood up very straight. "Yes, I have to go," I answered, pronouncing each word carefully. "I've got to go home and design a tiara. It's for Marguerite. I was at her party this afternoon. It was the best party I've ever been to. And Marguerite is the best friend I've ever had." Holding my kitten tightly against me, I turned and marched out of Sandy's house with my head held high.

11

Monday morning Jimmy Whaley tried to sit next to me on the bus. He'd almost missed it, and he was panting and clutching a piece of toast. "This seat is saved for Marguerite," I told him, loud enough for Sandy to hear.

"Marguerite?" said Jimmy Whaley. "What do you want to sit with *her* for?"

"She's my friend."

He gave me a puzzled look. "I thought Stork was your friend." He took a bite of his toast.

"I don't know anybody named Stork,"

I answered. "And you're getting crumbs all over this seat."

Jimmy shrugged and moved down the aisle.

When Marguerite got on, she sat right down next to me. Kristi squeezed in with us. We talked and laughed all the way to school. I talked the most and laughed the loudest. Loud enough for Sandy to hear.

I did the same thing at lunch and on the bus ride home. All day long I didn't look at Sandy once.

Tuesday I stuck with Marguerite again and we talked and laughed just like the day before. But this time I did look at Sandy. Once. In gym. We were doing folk dancing, and Marguerite picked me for her partner. We giggled as we swung each other around and around. "Oh, this is so much fun!" I shouted. I knew Sandy was dancing nearby with Paula, so I peeked over my shoulder. And she was looking right back at me with a sad expression on her face. She quickly turned her head away. Good, she's jealous, I said to myself, spinning Marguerite around fast. But I didn't really feel all that happy about it.

"Not so fast, Emma," Marguerite told me in her princessy way. "It isn't graceful. You must always dance gracefully."

"Oh, must I?" I said, making fun of the way she sounded.

She frowned at me and stopped dancing.

I didn't know whether Sandy was looking at us again, so I said, "Oh, you're so right, Marguerite. It's so important to be graceful."

Marguerite smiled, and I smiled too. We started dancing and giggling again like we were having the best time in the world. But I wasn't. I wasn't having a good time at all.

Wednesday wasn't very different from Tuesday—except Sandy and I looked at each other three times. Twice Sandy looked away first. Once I did.

Thursday during art the Scenery Committee started to work on the sets for the play. I was on the committee. Sandy was too. I was painting an igloo, and I needed the blue paint. Sandy had it in front of her. "Can I have the blue paint?" I asked her. It was the first thing I'd said to her since Sunday.

"Take it. I'll use the brown," she answered.

Our eyes met then, and neither of us

turned away. I remembered that day a year ago when we were both doing pictures of Thanksgiving turkeys. I could tell Sandy was remembering the same thing.

"Sandy . . ." I began.

But before I could say anything else, Marguerite came skipping over. She was wearing a new skirt that had so many ruffles on it, it looked like a pink wedding cake. "Oh, Emma, that set is going to be wonderful."

"Yeah," I said. I wanted her to disappear.

But she kept talking to me. "I know you'll do just as good a job on my crown after school today. I forgot to tell you— my mother said she'd pick up the silver glitter for you on her way home from work. We've already got the pipe cleaners."

"Great," I muttered. Go away, I thought.

She did, but not fast enough. When I turned back to Sandy, she was all the way on the other side of the room working with Paula. She didn't look my way again the rest of the day.

I was in a bad mood when Marguerite and I went to her house after school. Soon my bad mood got worse. I was having a hard time with Marguerite's crown. The pipe cleaners wouldn't twist just right. The glitter stuck more to my fingers than to the pipe cleaners. And Marguerite wasn't helping me at all. She just sat there next to me and told me how her ballet teacher said she was the most talented student in the class. Then she told me her coach had said the same thing. I didn't know what coach she was talking about. I thought maybe she'd taken up football or something.

She giggled. "Oh, Emma. You're so silly. My coach is my acting teacher. Do you really think *I'd* play football? It's a boys' game."

"I play football with my brother," I said in a grouchy voice. "So does Sandy McAllister."

"Well, I guess some girls like to do boy stuff," Marguerite replied. Maybe she was trying to be big minded. But it didn't sound that way.

"Not some girls. Lots of girls," I said. "And it's not *boy* stuff if girls like to do it. It's people stuff." I sounded a lot like my mom, and I waved the crown at Marguerite just the way Mom waves her fist when she's mad about something. A couple of the pipe cleaners untwisted.

"Watch it, Emma," warned Marguerite. "You're going to wreck my crown."

That's when, as Ronnie would say, I lost it. *My* crown, *my* crown," I mimicked. "If you're so worried about your dumb crown, why don't you make it yourself—instead of sitting there and telling me how great you are, Princess Marguerite?" I threw the crown down so hard, it flew apart, scattering pipe cleaners and glitter all over the place.

For a moment Marguerite stared at me as if I'd gone crazy. Then in a polite voice with icicles hanging from it, she said, "I think you'd better go home now, Emma."

Without saying a word, I turned and went.

12

Mom always says when you're really angry, a long, brisk walk will cool you off. So instead of waiting for Ms. Perrier to drive me home, I decided to take a very long, very brisk walk. But maybe it wasn't long or brisk enough, because when I got to my house, I wasn't cool at all. I was boiling.

I stomped into the kitchen. Everybody was already sitting at the dinner table. Go ahead, tell me I'm late. Just try it and see what happens, I thought.

But Dad was in a silly mood. He gets that way sometimes. "You're just in time," he said, "to sample the latest creation from Chef Richard Ames." He lifted the lid off the pot he was holding. *"Saucissons et haricots blancs en sauce tomate."*

"What's that?" I asked, with a frown.

"Franks and beans," Ronnie answered.

I frowned again and dropped into my seat.

Dad dished out the food. I moved it around on my plate. Dad saw me do it, but he didn't say anything.

Mom took a bite of her helping and told Dad it was very good. Then she started complaining about our neighbor, Mr. Murcheson. She said he was talking about cutting down the big old tree in his yard because it was giving too much shade. "That man. He doesn't care that a tree is a living thing, and that it's a home for other living things. All he cares about is getting a suntan. That man's

mind is smaller than small. It's . . .
it's . . ." She couldn't think of the word.

"Minuscule?" Dad suggested. "Micro-
scopic?"

"How about teensy-weensy?" Ronnie
put in.

Dad burst out laughing. Ronnie joined
in. "Very funny," said Mom. But she
chuckled too. I was the only one there
who didn't even crack a smile.

"Uh-oh," Dad said, looking at me.
"There's someone at this table who *really
doesn't* think we're funny."

I pushed the beans around my plate
some more and wouldn't look back at
him. I knew if I did I'd explode.

For a moment it was quiet in the
kitchen. Maybe they were all waiting
for me to laugh or tell them I did so
think they were funny. But I didn't open
my mouth.

Mom started talking again. "I nearly forgot to tell you what happened today at the library. As you know, I'm on the Activities Committee. Well, next month we're sponsoring a panel discussion, and I got to pick the topic."

"What is it?" asked Dad.

Mom paused, then proudly announced, " 'How to Be a Big-Minded Person in a Small-Minded World.' Now all I have to do is come up with the panel members."

"Why don't you pick Emma? She'd fit right in," Ronnie teased.

I stared at him. Hard.

Mom didn't seem to realize he was teasing. "You know, that's not such a bad idea," she said. "Emma could talk about her experience with the class play tryouts. How she chose to be big minded and vote for—"

99

She never got to finish the sentence, because I stood up and bellowed, "Mr. Murcheson isn't the one with the teensy-weensy mind! You are! You have the teensy-weensiest mind of all!" Then I ran out of the kitchen and up to my room as fast as I could.

13

I beat up my pillow for five whole minutes. I threw all my stuffed animals on the floor. I kicked the wall. Nothing helped. I was still mad.

Mom came up and tried to talk to me, but I refused to listen. Listening to her was what got me into trouble in the first place.

"Emma, you're being unreasonable. Tell me why you're so angry. Then I can tell you how to fix it," she pleaded through my closed door.

"You mean then you can tell me how

to make it worse!" I shouted back at her.

"Emma . . ."

"Go away!"

Dad tried next. But I wouldn't talk to him either. I just sat there cuddling Cinnamon, my kitten. There was only one person I wanted to talk or listen to—and she didn't want to talk or listen to me.

I felt my eyes get hot and watery. I was going to cry. I didn't want to cry. I put the cat on the floor and grabbed my pillow again to beat it.

Suddenly something went *ping* in my head. I jumped up and dropped my pillow. I ran over to my desk and took out a large white pad of paper and a pen. I wrote seven words across the top of the first sheet, then read what I'd written:

Twenty Ways to Lose Your Best Friend
Then I began.

I worked on the list for a long time.
First I put down all the things I'd done
to Sandy. Then I put down the things
Sandy had done to me. After that I
thought about things that would've made
me mad if Sandy had done them, and
stuff that would've made Sandy mad if
I had. All together that made nineteen

things. But no matter how hard I tried, I couldn't think of the twentieth thing. I put my head down on my desk to rest for a while, and before I knew it, I fell asleep.

When I woke up, it was midnight. My neck was stiff and my shoulders were too, and I still couldn't think of one more thing to finish the list. I yawned and stretched and paced around my room. I opened my door a crack and listened. It was totally quiet. Mom and Dad and Ronnie had all gone to bed. I went back to my desk and stared down at the list once more. The blank space next to number twenty looked very big and white. I sighed. Then, with a shrug, I scooped up the paper and folded it in half. I folded it again and put it in a big white envelope. On the envelope I wrote three words: "For Sandy McAllister." Then I added "Only."

With the envelope in my hand I walked over to my door and listened once more. It was just as quiet as before. Holding my breath, I eased the door open wide enough to slip through. Cinnamon tried to come out too, but I pushed her gently inside. Then I tiptoed down the stairs and out the back door.

I am a fast runner, and the chilly air and darkness made me run even faster. Before you could say "Marguerite Perrier," I was shoving the envelope under the door to Sandy's house. And before you could say "Sandy McAllister," I was back at my house again and in my bed. What did I just do? I wondered. But I didn't wonder too long. I fell asleep instead.

14

I didn't want to get out of bed the next morning. If I got out of bed, I'd have to go downstairs. If I went downstairs, I'd have to go to school. If I went to school, I'd have to see Sandy. If I saw Sandy, I'd find out whether or not she was really going to hate me forever. And if I found out that she was going to hate me forever, I'd go back to my room, get into my bed, and never leave it again.

I covered my head with my pillow and heard someone open my door and come over to my bed. "Wake up, Sleeping Ugly," Ronnie sang out.

"Get lost," I told him.

"Mom and Dad have already left for work. My orders are to get you out of bed—*any way I can.*" He sat down on my ankles and began to tickle my feet.

"No!" I tried to kick at him. But he wouldn't budge.

I'm very ticklish, and soon I was laughing and crying and promising I'd get up if only he'd stop.

He did, and I swung my pillow at him. But he grabbed it and bopped me back. Then we wrestled on my bed like we used to do when we were smaller.

"You're pretty tough, Sleeping Ugly," Ronnie said, flopping down on his back.

"You bet I am!" I said, lying next to him.

"But not that tough. If you were really that tough, you'd get up, go to school, and find out what Sandy thinks of the message you delivered to her house last night."

"What! How do you know I delivered something to—" I stopped talking when I saw the big grin on Ronnie's face. "You sneak! You creep! You were spying on me!"

"I wasn't spying. I was outside by the garbage cans trying to fish out my *Teen Mutants* comic. Mom threw it away last night after you told her what a teensy-weensy mind she has and I laughed. You ran right past me with a big white envelope in your hand. Straight to Sandy's house. I hope you didn't write and tell her she has a teensy-weensy mind too."

I glared at him. "No, I didn't. But

if you think I am going to tell you what I did write, you're crazy. I wouldn't tell you that if you tickled my feet for three hours."

"Oh, yeah? We'll see about that." He made a grab for my feet, but I jumped off the bed.

He grinned again. "Mission accomplished. I got you out of bed." He got up too, tucked his shirt into his pants, and headed for the door. Just as he got there, he called over his shoulder, "Good luck today, Emma."

I stared after him, surprised. "Thanks," I said. He was already gone, but it didn't matter. I kind of think he heard me anyway. Then I started to get dressed.

I missed the bus and had to walk all the way to school. When I started out,

I felt brave. I am tough, I kept telling myself. I *am* tough.

But by the time I got to school, I wasn't feeling so brave anymore. I was late. I knew everyone would stare at me or make some remark when I came in and Ms. Wood would be annoyed. And that's exactly what happened. Marguerite, Kristi, and Jeanine stared at me and turned up their noses. Jimmy Whaley called out, "What happened, Emma? Did your alarm clock break?" Ms. Wood said, "You're late, Emma. We're having a spelling test." I couldn't even look at Sandy. I was too scared.

I slumped in my seat. For the rest of the morning, I didn't pay any attention to Ms. Wood or anybody else. I spent all the time trying not to cry.

Lunchtime came. I went and hid in the girls' room. I thought about leaving school and going home, but I didn't want to get in trouble. So when lunch period ended, I went back to my classroom and slumped down in my seat again.

"Take out your math workbooks," Ms. Wood said.

Mine was in my desk. I pulled it out. When I opened it up, something fell on the floor. It was a big white envelope. On the front it had said "For Sandy McAllister Only," but now "Sandy McAllister" was crossed out and it read "For Emma Ames Only." I opened the envelope, careful not to let Ms. Wood see, took out the piece of paper that was inside, and let out a big, sad sigh. It was my list. The one I'd delivered to Sandy last night. She was delivering it right back to me. I sighed again. What a stupid idea. Did I really think giving Sandy that list would work? I started to crumple it up when something made me look down at the paper once more. Last night there were only nineteen things on the list. Today there were twenty. The twentieth thing was in Sandy's handwriting. I read it slowly. "The twentieth way to lose your best friend," it said, "is not to help your best friend come up with the twentieth way to lose your best friend."

"Huh?" I said out loud.

"Are you having a problem, Emma?" asked Ms. Wood.

"Oh, no!" I told her quickly, covering the list with my hand. Ms. Wood turned back to the blackboard, and I read what Sandy had written again and then once more. And I started to laugh. I looked over at Sandy. She was looking back at me, and she was laughing too.

"What's going on here? Emma? Sandy?" Ms. Wood asked sternly.

But that only made us laugh harder.

"Go out into the hall until you can control yourselves," Ms. Wood ordered.

Out into the hall we went—and laughed and laughed until we couldn't laugh anymore.

"You're not really friends with Princess Marguerite, are you?" Sandy asked.

"No way. Are you really friends with Paula?"

"Well, actually . . . yes. I am. I like her. But not as much as you. She's not my best friend. And I'm sorry I showed our kitten-name list to her when I promised not to show it to anybody. That wasn't right."

"I'm sorry I tried to make you jealous of Marguerite. That wasn't right either."

"I'm sorry I wouldn't talk to you when you voted for Marguerite," Sandy said, and waited.

I knew what she was waiting for. She was waiting for me to say I was sorry I'd voted for Marguerite instead of her. I *wanted* to say it. But I couldn't. Do I really think I did the wrong thing? I wondered. Then, slowly and softly, I said, "Sandy. I know you want me to say I shouldn't have voted for Marguerite. I know you want me to apologize. But I can't. I really thought she was the best person for the part. And I really believe you should vote for the best person, even if you don't like her a whole lot. There are other things *you're* the best person for, and if you were trying out for one of those things, I'd vote for you. What I am sorry about is that I didn't tell you that right away. Maybe then you wouldn't have gotten so mad at me."

Sandy thought for a while too, and finally shook her head. "I still would've gotten mad. I still *am* mad. But I guess I sort of understand."

We stood there feeling kind of shy. I think we wanted to hug each other, but we couldn't. Not yet.

Jimmy Whaley stuck his head out the door. "Ms. Wood says you two can come back in now."

"We're coming," I said.

"Hey, are you and Emma friends again, Stork?" Jimmy asked.

Without looking at him Sandy said, "If there were an election right now, I know who the best person for Class Pain would be."

I started to laugh again. So did Sandy. Ms. Wood wouldn't let us back in the room for another fifteen minutes.

15

It's funny how a day can start so bad and finish so good. Sandy and I are friends again. I'm pretty sure we'll stay that way for a long time. In fact, the President of the United States himself couldn't stop us from being friends now, even if he wanted to.

Sandy and I spent the whole afternoon together working on a new list: Twenty-Five Things We Can Do Better Than Marguerite Perrier. It was a fun list to write. Too bad Marguerite won't get to read it. She might learn something—but I doubt it.

I left Sandy's house just in time for dinner. Mom, Dad, and Ronnie were already sitting at the table just the way they'd been the night before. But this time I didn't wait for anyone to ask me anything. "Did Ronnie tell you where I was?" I burst out. "I was at Sandy's house! We're friends again!"

"That's great, Emma," Dad said.

Ronnie looked up from his comic, wiggled his eyebrows at me, and went back to reading.

Only Mom didn't say anything. She didn't talk through dinner either. She looked sad, and like she wanted me to say something to her. I remembered how mad I'd been at her the night before and what I'd said. That was it. Mom wanted me to apologize.

I waited until we finished eating. "I'll

dry the dishes tonight if you wash, Mom," I said, grabbing a towel.

For a while we worked quietly. Then I said, "Mom, I'm really sorry I told you you have a teensy-weensy mind. You don't—at least not most of the time."

Mom's lips twitched. "I think that was an apology. Therefore I think I'll accept it." She handed me another dish to dry.

A moment later she said, "I'm glad you and Sandy are friends again. Nancy McAllister and I had a long talk about you girls today. I think Nancy finally saw my point of view just the way Sandy saw yours."

"Oh Mom, that's great! That means you and Ms. McAllister are friends again."

Mom paused. Then she said, "Not exactly."

"What do you mean, not exactly?"

"Well, as I said, we were talking about you and Sandy and the class play. Nancy thinks you kids shouldn't vote on who gets what part at all. She thinks your teacher should simply hand out the roles. I don't agree with her. I think that's very undemocratic. I think it's small minded. *Very* small minded. And that's what I told Nancy."

"Oh, Mom. Not again." I sighed.

"I'm afraid so," she replied, so low I could hardly hear it. She looked down at the sink. "You know, I really miss talking to her, even if we don't agree on everything. I wish we were friends again."

For a minute neither of us said anything. Then I began to smile. "Listen,

Mom, you want me to help you fix it this time?"

Mom raised her head. "You? How? How could you fix it?"

"Get some paper and a pen," I said. "We're going to write a little list."